The Adventure of the Empty House

By Arthur Conan Doyle

Adapted by David Eastman

Illustrated by Allan Eitzen

TROLL ASSOCIATES

Library of Congress Cataloging in Publication Data

Eastman, David.
    Sherlock Holmes—The adventure of the empty
house.

    Summary: Sherlock Holmes is thought to be dead,
murdered by his enemy Moriarty, but turns up alive
to solve a puzzling murder.
    [1. Mystery and detective stories] I. Doyle,
Arthur Conan, Sir, 1859-1930. Adventure of
the empty house. II. Eitzen, Allan, ill.
III. Title.
PZ7.E1269Ad   [Fic]   81-11673
ISBN 0-89375-616-4   AACR2
ISBN 0-89375-617-2 (pbk.)

Printed in the United States of America
10 9 8 7 6 5 4 3 2 1

Because of my close friendship with Mr. Sherlock Holmes, I became deeply interested in unsolved crimes. After his death, I even tried to solve a few mysteries myself—by using his methods of observation and deduction. One case that especially appealed to me was the murder of Ronald Adair. As I read the strange and mysterious facts of the case, I wished Holmes were still alive.

Ronald Adair was a highly respected young man. He had no enemies or bad habits that anyone knew of. He often played cards, but never for stakes that would hurt him. Some weeks before his death, he had won a large amount of money playing with Colonel Moran as his partner. On the day of his death, he had lost a small amount playing with Colonel Moran, Mr. Murray, and Sir John Hardy.

That night, he was found lying on the floor of his room with a soft-nosed revolver bullet in his head. No weapon was found. On the table were neat stacks of money and a sheet of paper on which he had written some figures and the names of some friends. Perhaps he had been trying to figure out his losses or winnings.

The door had been locked from the inside. The window was open, but it was two stories above the ground. Directly below it was a flower bed, which had not been disturbed. The street where Adair lived was a busy one, but no one had heard a shot fired. Yet a revolver bullet was in the man's head.

6

The next evening, I went to the scene of the crime. A detective was there, making foolish observations. As I turned to go, I bumped into an old man, whose back was stooped and bent. Some books he was carrying dropped to the ground. I picked them up and apologized, but he snatched them from me and disappeared with a snarl.

No sooner had I returned home, when my maid showed the same old man into my study. He spoke in a strange, croaking voice. "I wanted to apologize for being so gruff, and to thank you for picking up my books," he said. Then he pointed behind me and added, "You could use a few more books yourself—to fill that gap on the second shelf."

I glanced at my bookshelf. When I looked back, Sherlock Holmes stood before me.

"I am glad to be out of that uncomfortable disguise," he said. I immediately fainted. When I awoke, Holmes was bending over me. "My dear Watson," he said, "I owe you an apology. I had no idea you would react that way."

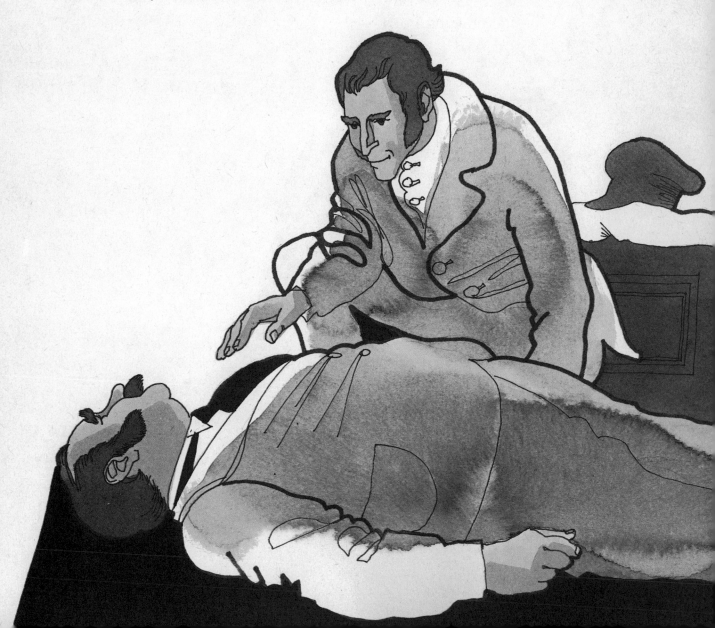

"Holmes!" I cried. "How can it be you? You tumbled into that deep gorge in the Swiss Alps!"

"Not quite," he replied. "I struggled at the edge with my enemy, Professor Moriarty, but I managed to break free. He alone plunged into the gorge."

"But the footprints!" I cried. "Two sets went down the path, and none returned."

"This is what happened," explained Holmes. "I reasoned that if I let my other enemies think I was dead, I might be able to catch them off guard and destroy them, too. So I found a few footholds in the wall behind me and climbed up to a ledge, where I hid.

"I lay there until you had left, and until the official investigation was complete. Suddenly, a huge rock fell from above and nearly landed on me. Looking up, I saw a man's head. Then another stone came toward me. Clearly, Moriarty had not been alone. Now his companion was trying to finish the job of killing me.

"I knew that I had to flee. Another stone whipped by me as I hung by my hands from the ledge. Halfway down, I slipped, but I landed on the path. As quickly as I could, I ran through the mountains for at least ten miles in the darkness. The next morning, I continued on my way. A week later, I reached Italy.

13

"As you know, the trial of Moriarty's gang left two dangerous men at large. I could not safely return to London, so I traveled for a few years. After some time, I learned that only one of my old enemies was still alive. Then I heard about the strange murder of Ronald Adair. I knew that the time had come for me to return. This afternoon, I visited my old offices at Baker Street. Tonight, we will start on the adventure of the empty house."

That evening, Holmes led me through a path of alleys and passages that I did not even know existed. He took great care to see that we were not followed. Finally, we reached the back door of a deserted house.

Inside, we felt our way through the darkness. The wallpaper hung in ribbons from the walls. We crept down a long, dark hall. Then Holmes turned to the right and entered a large, empty room. There was no lamp, and the window was thick with dust.

"We are directly opposite my office at Baker Street," whispered my friend. I looked toward the window of his office and gave a cry of amazement. Holmes—or someone who looked just like him—was sitting in a chair before the window. I reached out to make sure he was really still next to me.

"That looks just like you!" I exclaimed.

"It is a specially made wax dummy," whispered Holmes. "My old enemies saw me arrive this morning. By tonight, the most dangerous criminal in London—the same man who dropped the rocks over the cliff—will be after me. But he will not know that *we* are after *him*."

I began to see what my friend's plan was. The dummy in the
office window was the bait. We were the hunters. And our prey
was the man who was after Holmes. We waited and watched. I
noticed two suspicious figures huddled in a doorway up the
street. I drew Holmes's attention to them, but he was not at all
interested. Later, I learned that they were the police.

Suddenly I whispered, "Holmes! The dummy moved!"

"Of course," scoffed Holmes. "Otherwise, it would fool no one. My housekeeper—Mrs. Hudson—is up there. She is lying on the floor. She moves the dummy from time to time." The street outside was empty and silent. Suddenly, Holmes pulled me back into a corner and pressed his hand over my mouth. A door quietly opened and shut at the back of the house. A moment later, footsteps came down the hall.

The vague outline of a man crept into the room. The dark figure went to the window and noiselessly opened it. Then he assembled a strange-looking rifle and loaded it. With the barrel resting on the windowsill, he took aim.

The gunman's finger slowly tightened on the trigger. Then there was a strange whizzing sound and the tinkle of broken glass. Holmes sprang onto the man's back and pushed his face to the floor. A moment later, the gunman had seized Holmes by the throat. I struck him with my revolver, and he dropped to the floor.

There was the clatter of running feet on the pavement outside. Two police officers rushed through the front door and into the darkened room. With them was a plainclothes detective.

"Is that you, Lestrade?" called Holmes.

"Yes, Mr. Holmes," he replied. "I took the job myself. Good to see you back in London, sir."

"I thought you needed a little unofficial help," said Holmes.

As the police lighted their lanterns, Holmes said, "Gentlemen, meet Colonel Sebastian Moran. The last time I saw him was when I lay on a ledge in the Swiss Alps."

"You fiend," muttered the prisoner.

Holmes picked up the air rifle and said, "A unique weapon— noiseless and powerful. I knew it had been built for the late Professor Moriarty, but I have never seen it until now." He inspected the rifle closely.

"Just as I thought," he said. "It uses special, soft-nosed bullets. Tell me, Lestrade—what charge will be brought against Moran?"

"Why, the attempted murder of Sherlock Holmes, of course," replied Lestrade.

"Not so," said Holmes. "I wish to keep my name out of this."

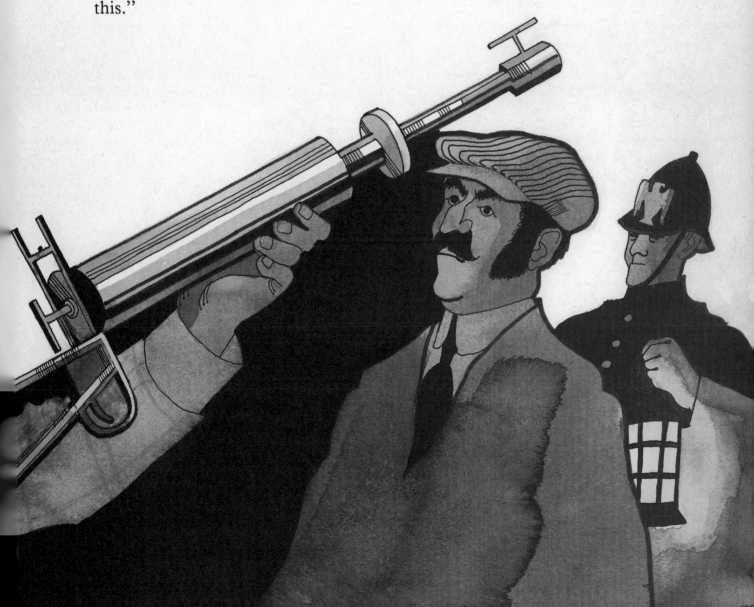

Lestrade was puzzled. "Then what charge—?"

"Murder," replied Holmes. "Colonel Moran shot Ronald Adair with a soft-nosed bullet, fired from this air rifle, through an open second-floor window. That's the charge, Lestrade. Now, Watson, if you will come with me, I will try to explain what has taken place."

As we entered his office, Holmes said, "Well done, Mrs. Hudson. Did you happen to see where the bullet went?"

"It passed right through the head of your wax dummy," she said, "and flattened itself against the wall. Here it is."

"They were clever," said Holmes. "Who would expect a soft-nosed revolver bullet to be fired from a powerful air rifle?

27

"You see, Watson," Holmes explained, "Colonel Moran was an excellent shot. Professor Moriarty used him in only one or two difficult jobs. Three years ago, he and Moriarty followed us to Switzerland. Moriarty tried to kill me, but fell to his own death. Then Moran tried to kill me, but I escaped.

28

"Unfortunately, I had no proof, so Moran remained free," said Holmes. "My chance to put him behind bars came when I read about the death of Ronald Adair. I knew at once that Moran was the murderer. It was clear to me that he had played cards with Adair, followed him home, and shot him through the open window.

"I came back to London, knowing that Moran would try to get me out of the way at once. But instead of killing me, he fell right into my trap and was captured."

"What was Moran's motive for killing Adair?" I asked.

"Moran and Adair had won a large amount of money playing cards together as partners," said Holmes. "But Moran had probably cheated.

"Adair must have threatened to expose the Colonel unless he resigned from the club where they played cards. That would have ruined Moran, so he murdered Adair."

"How do you explain the stacks of money and the list of names?" I asked.

"Adair was probably trying to work out how much of his winnings he should return himself," explained Holmes.

"At any rate, Watson," said my friend, "Colonel Moran will trouble us no more. The famous air rifle will be placed in Scotland Yard Museum, and once again Mr. Sherlock Holmes is free to devote his life to solving those interesting little problems that fill the lives of the people of London."